Text copyright © 1996 Herbie Brennan
Illustrations copyright © 1996 Stephen Lewis

First published in Great Britain in 1996
by Macdonald Young Books Ltd
Campus 400
Maylands Avenue
Hemel Hempstead
Herts HP2 7EZ

Designed and Typeset by Backup... Design and Production.
Printed and bound in Belgium by Proost N.V.

British Library Cataloguing in Publication Data available.

ISBN: 0 7500 1952 2

ISBN: 0 7500 1953 0

HERBIE BRENNAN

Little House

Illustrated by Stephen Lewis

MACDONALD YOUNG BOOKS

For Aynia with much love

Chapter One

"Drawing!" Mr Miller scowled. He began to hand out sheets of paper and large, soft pencils.

"If it was up to me," he said, "I'd give you sums all day." He snorted. "Drawing – ha! What good did drawing ever do for anybody?"

Tilly didn't know, but she knew she liked drawing. It helped her forget how horrible school was now she'd moved into Mr Miller's class.

"You have an hour to do your ghastly drawings," Mr Miller said. "Anything you like – it doesn't matter since they'll be useless anyway. Then," he smiled grimly, "I'll give you sums."

He went back behind his desk and glared. "And no rubbing out with your finger! It makes a dreadful mess."

"But, sir," protested Simon Walker, who was very brave, "we don't have any proper rubbers."

"Anybody who needs a rubber can borrow the one on my desk," said Mr Miller. He glared again. "If he dares!"

Tilly stared at the sheet of paper. She decided she really hated Mr Miller. She'd been happy at school when she was in Mrs Wilson's class. And even happier

when she moved into Miss Roberts' class. But Mr Miller was so bad tempered all the time he made her life a misery. And everybody in the class felt exactly the same way.

After a while, she lifted her pencil and began to draw.

Chapter Two

Tilly drew a dear sweet little house with a high pointed roof and two chimneys. She swirled the tip of her pencil around one of the chimneys to make smoke.

She drew two windows, like eyes, on the front of the house. She drew a door, like a nose, between them.

Tilly stared at the house. It was happening the way it always happened when she began to draw. She started to see the little house in her mind as if it was real.

She could imagine a garden around it and a winding path right up to the front door. She could imagine trees and a back yard with hens scratching in the dirt. She could imagine a little shed to one side. She could imagine a lion knocker on the door.

Tilly drew the knocker on the door. She couldn't manage the lion's head, so she made do with an ordinary knocker. She drew the winding path and put in bushy shapes as garden shrubs. She  drew trees with a hammock slung between them. She tried to draw the shed and while it ended up leaning quite a bit to one side, it didn't look too bad. She added a latch and a large black bolt to the shed door.

She drew a sun above the house, with lines coming out of it for rays. On impulse, she drew a cat in the garden, sunning itself.

The cat didn't turn out well. It looked lopsided and wicked and far too large, but she was afraid to go up to Mr Miller's desk to borrow the rubber, so she left it in.

She thought perhaps her drawing was finished. Since there was still most of the hour left, she propped her head on her hand, stared at her little house, and began to doze.

Chapter Three

Tilly opened her eyes with a jerk and knew at once something was wrong.

She was no longer in class. She was in an empty room with a wood fire burning in the grate. There was no furniture of any sort, no pictures hanging on the walls, no carpet nor even linoleum on the floor.

And she was completely, utterly alone.

Tilly looked round fearfully. The inside of the room was white – walls, floor and ceiling – like a hospital. It felt really creepy. And what was most creepy was that there was something missing.

Of course there was something missing! Everything was missing. The furniture was missing. The pictures were missing. The carpet was
miss …

But she knew it was more than that. She knew she had never been in a room like this before and didn't quite know why. She looked around again and still couldn't work it out.

She looked through the window. There was a little garden outside with a winding path and some very pretty shrubs. She could see a hammock slung between two chestnut trees.

Where was she? Frowning, Tilly looked around a third time. There was still no clue to where she was or how she got here. She glanced back out through the window and decided if she went out into the garden, she might find somebody who could help her.

She made to leave the room and suddenly realised what was missing.

There was no door, no door at all.

She was trapped.

Chapter Four

Heart thumping, Tilly began to make her
way around the walls, feeling them
carefully with her hands, peering closely at
the dead white surface.

All four walls were smooth. There was
not a crack, not a sign of a door anywhere,
not a sign there ever had been a door. But
who would build a room without a door?

And how had she got in here if not through a door?

Through the window!

Of course through the window!

Tilly ran to the window. There was no clasp, no sash, no fixings of any sort. She tried to push it up, but it did not move. She tried to open it outwards, but it would not open. In desperation she began to pound it with her fists, but it would not break.

Tilly backed away from the window in horror. She did not know where she was. She did not know how she got here. She did not know how to get out.

The chimney! She could climb up the chimney!

It wasn't something she would normally have done, but in a room without a door and a window that wouldn't open, there was nothing else for it. She ran to the fireplace, but the logs were still burning brightly. She could not climb up the chimney without setting herself on fire.

"Help," squeaked Tilly, close to tears.

There was a huge crash as the window smashed and a monster burst into the room.

Chapter Five

Tilly spun round.

The monster looked a bit like a cat, but it was like no cat she'd ever seen. It was larger than a leopard, larger than a lion. It was lopsided and distorted with a wicked look in its eye.

"Miaow!" it said.
Tilly ran.

She ran round the empty room because there was nowhere else to run. The great lopsided cat leaped after her as if she were a mouse.

"Leave me alone!" screamed Tilly.

The great cat swatted with its claws and came so close she heard the *swish* beside her ear. She ran even harder.

"Miaow!" the great cat said again.

Tilly ran twice round the room with the great cat getting closer and closer until she could feel its hot breath on her neck.

Huge paws lashed out time and time again, missing her by inches, then by an inch, then half an inch, a quarter, an eighth, a sixteenth ...

The window was open!

The great cat had burst in through the window, smashing it to pieces.

There was now a huge jagged hole in the wall as if somebody had punched through paper.

As the great cat swatted her one final time, Tilly dived through the hole.

Chapter Six

She was in a garden.

The house behind her had two windows, like eyes (one of them now a gaping hole) and a front door like a nose. There was a knocker on the door, but it was not a lion knocker. A path wound its way towards the house. There were bushy shrubs beside it.

Tilly looked round at the trees with the hammock slung between them, saw the shed leaning a little to one side. Somehow she knew that if she went round the back, she would find a yard with hens scratching in the dirt.

Was she dreaming? She didn't think so. Somehow she had fallen into her own drawing of the dear sweet little house. It was the only thing that made sense. Everything she'd drawn was here – the high pointed roof, the smoke swirling from the chimney – but more to the point, the things she *hadn't* drawn were *not* here.

Which explained, as she now noticed, that the front door had no handle.

Which explained why the room inside had no door!

Tilly looked at the house

and garden in amazement. It was terrible, but it was wonderful. It was her drawing come to life!

A great lopsided shape leaped through the broken window.

"Miaow!" it said. "Miaow! Miaow!"

Tilly wished she hadn't drawn the stupid cat.

Chapter Seven

Tilly ran into the bushes. The great cat followed. She ran around the trees. The great cat followed. She ran around the house into the back yard. Hens scattered in all directions.

The hens distracted the great cat which began to chase them wildly. Tilly seized her opportunity to race off back to the front of her little house.

She knew the great cat would soon tire of chasing the hens and come after her again, but at least it would give her time to think. She rested against the wall of the house and thought.

Since she'd forgotten to draw a handle on the front door, she couldn't go inside, except through the broken window which only led back into the empty room. She thought briefly of climbing a tree, but all cats could climb as well, so that wouldn't do her much good.

Her eye fell on the shed.

It leaned a little, but it looked very strong. There was a window, but it was a tiny window, far too small for the great cat to squeeze through. And best of all, there was a large black latch on the door, which meant she could open it and, more importantly, close it behind her.

The screeching of the hens stopped suddenly. Since the great cat couldn't possibly have caught them all, it meant the cat had tired of chasing them.

In the sudden silence, it was padding round the house, sniffing the air and trying to find her.

Tilly ran towards the shed.

Chapter Eight

The great cat bounded round the side of
the house. It stopped and swung its great
lopsided head to and fro, searching. Its
wicked eyes gleamed.

It walked to the ruined window of the
house and looked inside. There was no
little girl in the empty room.

It looked through the other window, just in case she had managed to get into the house some other way. There was no little girl in that room either.

The great cat turned and stared around the garden. Like all cats it had amazing eyesight. There was no little girl hiding in the bushes, no little girl running down the winding path.

It looked at the hammock, which was empty of any little girl. It stared up into the trees in case she had been foolish enough to climb. There was no little girl in the trees.

Then suddenly it noticed the shed.

There was a pink ribbon hanging from the latch, very like the ribbon the little girl had worn in her hair. And best of all, the ribbon had caught in the latch so the shed door was not closed properly!

The great cat hurled itself towards the shed. The shed door slammed open as the great cat hit it and with a howl of triumph the great cat disappeared inside.

At once Tilly appeared from behind the shed. Before the great cat knew what was

happening, she
slammed the door
and shot the bolt in
place.

The great cat
went crazy inside
the shed, scratching and spitting and
howling.

But it couldn't get out.

Chapter Nine

Tilly wondered how she was going to get back to her classroom.

She sat in the sunshine while the great cat caterwauled, and thought about it deeply.

She remembered drawing the house, but couldn't recall how she got here. She remembered looking at her drawing, but couldn't recall how she got here. She remembered resting her head on her hand.

She'd fallen asleep! That was how she'd got here! Somehow in her sleep, she'd left the real world of the classroom and entered the flat world of her drawing. She was certain that was how it had happened.

An idea occurred to her. She glanced at the hammock, but did not climb in. There was something she wanted to check on first.

Tilly walked down the winding garden path away from the house. The howls of the great cat faded slowly behind her. She reached the end of the path eventually.

Things were exactly as she'd thought they might be. The path ended in an enormous drawing of her classroom with its desks and its blackboard and even the

view of the playground through the window. There were drawings of all the children and, behind a drawing of his desk, a rather nasty drawing of Mr Miller.

43

Tilly smiled. The first time she slept, her drawing had become the real world and the real world had become a drawing! If she slept again, her drawing would once again become a drawing and the real world would once again become real.

But before she slept, there was
something she had to do.

Tilly reached up to the drawing of the
real world and, using her finger, carefully
rubbed out Mr Miller.

Then she walked back up the path,
climbed into the hammock and, despite
the howling of the great cat, fell
instantly asleep.

Look out for more creepy titles in the Shivery Storybooks series:

The Ghost Bus by Anthony Masters

When Jack and Tina catch a late bus home from school, they very quickly realise that this is no ordinary bus. For a start, it's distinctly old fashioned, but worse, they can see right through their fellow passengers! They're on a ghost bus, a ghost bus with a mission...

The Bugman by Andrew Donkin

Justin is a bully. But one day he underestimates one of his victims, or rather a whole colony of them. It's Justin's turn to be afraid when the bugs get their horrifying revenge...

Time Flies by Mary Hooper

When Lucy hides in the wooden chest at the old manor house, it's just a game. But then she gets the fright of her life when she opens the lid and discovers that everything has changed. Somehow she has gone back to Tudor times and now she's trapped in a strange and terrifying world...

All these books and many more in the Storybooks series can be purchased from your local bookseller. For more information about Storybooks, write to: *The Sales Department, Macdonald Young Books, Campus 400, Maylands Avenue, Hemel Hempstead HP2 7EZ.*